Sofia and the Heartmender

Written and Illustrated by
Marie Olofsdotter

HOLY COW! PRESS · DULUTH, MINNESOTA

Holy Cow! Press edition ISBN 978-0-9779458-3-2.
Design preparation by Clarity (Duluth, Minnesota).
Printed in China by Morris Press LTD and Creative Printing USA.

10 9 8 7 6 5 4 3 2 1

Library of Congress Cataloging-in-Publication Data

Olofsdotter, Marie
Sofia and the Heartmender / written and illustrated by Marie Olofsdotter.
p.   cm.
Summary: When no one seems to understand Sofia's fear of the shadow-monsters that
she sees in the dark, her heart breaks and she goes to see the Heartmender for help.
ISBN 0-915793-50-4
[1. Fear of the dark — Fiction. 2. Night — Fiction.] I. Title.
PZ7.05165So 1993
[E] — dc20   92-46200
CIP   AC

The color illustrations are color pencil on textured heavyweight watercolor papers; black and white illustrations
are black ink on scratchboard. The display type is Metropolis and Metropolis Shaded; the text type is Belucian.

This project is funded in part by a grant from the Alan H. Zeppa Family Foundation,
with additional support provided by individual donors.

Holy Cow! Press books are distributed to the trade by Consortium Book Sales & Distribution,
c/o Perseus Distribution, 1094 Flex Drive, Jackson, Tennessee 38301.

For personal inquiries, write to:
Holy Cow! Press
Post Office Box 3170
Mount Royal Station
Duluth, Minnesota 55803
Please visit our website: www.holycowpress.org

I dedicate this book to the Mystery,
my family,
and all the Heartmenders in my life.

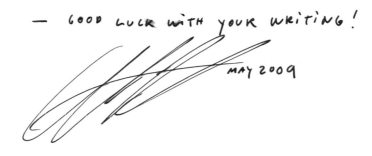

ANV KALLi !

☰♡☰

— GOOD LUCK WITH YOUR WRITING !

MAY 2009

Sofia sat in her room looking out her window at the horizon. "When the edge turns pink, the shadow-monsters come," she said to her cat. "We'd better keep the lamp on all night."

"Go to bed, Sofia," said a voice from the living room. "And turn off your light."

"I want my light on," Sofia answered.

"Don't be stubborn," the voice said, sounding angry now.

Sofia watched the pink line on the horizon disappear in the night. She crawled into her bed and pulled the blanket over her head.

Footsteps came towards her room. The feet stopped and the light was turned off. "Good night," said an impatient voice.

Sofia heard the feet go back into the living room. All night long, the shadow-monsters danced on the walls. They appeared in every corner and filled the whole room. Sofia did not get much sleep.

In the morning, in front of the mirror, she saw a crack in her heart. She stood still for a moment, then put on her clothes and walked into the kitchen.

Sofia looked at her egg and toast. "I don't want to eat," she said.

"You have to eat," her mother answered. "Everybody has to eat breakfast. And don't start talking about shadow-monsters again—they don't exist. It's silly to be afraid of the dark."

When nobody was watching, Sofia put her egg and toast into her school bag. She went to the hallway to put on her jacket. Stopping in front of the hallway mirror, she saw that the crack in her heart had grown longer and wider.

"Get to school," her father yelled. "You're late."

In school, the first assignment was drawing. Sofia's head was full of shadow-monsters. She started drawing them to get them out. None of them would fit on one piece of paper. They grew bigger and bigger, and Sofia needed more and more paper to draw them.

"Stop!" her teacher commanded. "You are wasting all that paper! What are those things, anyway? Didn't you hear the assignment? You are supposed to be drawing spring flowers."

Sofia heard a crack. She looked down at the floor. There was her heart, lying by her feet in two pieces.

Everybody else was busy drawing flowers. The teacher was busy helping them. Nobody saw Sofia pick up the halves of her heart, put them into her bag, and leave school.

Sofia sat down on a rock and closed her eyes. Suddenly she felt something sniffing her toes. She opened her eyes and saw a dog. "So, what are you going to do with your broken heart?" the dog asked her.

"I don't know," Sofia answered. "Can you tell me where to find a Heartmender?"

"I can tell you," said the dog, "but you will have to draw a map."

"My teacher says that I shouldn't waste paper," Sofia replied. "She thinks that I am not very good at drawing."

The dog looked at her. "Drawing is not a matter of paper or what teachers think. Close your eyes and draw a map inside your eyelids. Then you will always know where it is, and you will never lose it."

Sofia closed her eyes and listened carefully to what the dog told her. She looked at her eyelids and knew just what to do. When she opened her eyes, the dog was gone.

Sofia followed her eye map. She walked all day. Just as the sun was setting, she reached the edge of a forest. Sofia closed her eyes, but now all she could see was darkness. Frightened, she opened her eyes quickly. The dog was sitting in front of her.

"I am glad you are here," she said. "What do I do now? I can't see anything on my eyelids, and I am afraid of the dark." Sofia told the dog about the shadow-monsters that came to her room at night.

"They visit you because they are hungry and lonely," the dog told her. "Look straight at them, and give them something to eat. Then tell them to leave you alone unless they have something important to say. The night is your friend. In the dark is where seeds grow and dreams live." The dog handed Sofia a flashlight. "The Heartmender lives in the middle of the forest," he said.

Sofia thanked the dog and started walking. She walked slowly at first, then faster and faster as she felt less and less afraid. She had been walking for an hour when she came to a clearing. In the center stood a little house. "That must be the Heartmender's house," she said to her cat. She took a step towards it.

All at once, the shadow-monsters appeared. They lined up like a fence in front of the house. Sofia was very frightened. She fell backwards, dropping her flashlight and her bag. She lay on her back a few seconds.

Suddenly Sofia was furious. How dare the shadow-monsters block her way to the Heartmender's house!

Sofia jumped up and looked straight at the shadow-monsters. "What do you want?" she demanded. The shadow-monsters swayed slowly from side to side but did not answer.

Sofia stomped her foot on the ground. "Tell me!" The shadow-monsters swayed nervously from side to side. They did not look scary anymore. They looked lost and helpless.

Sofia remembered what the dog had told her. She took the egg and toast out of her bag and set them on the ground. "You can have this," she said. "Then leave me alone unless you have something important to say." The shadow-monsters bowed to her in unison. They all bent down at the same time to eat the food. Their heads slammed together, and the shadow-monsters fell to the ground. They raised their heads, looking surprised and sleepy at the same time, then started to fade. Sofia giggled to herself and watched them disappear. When they were gone, she walked up to the house in the clearing.

Her friend the dog was lying on the doorstep. "The Heartmender is waiting for you," he said. Sofia handed him the flashlight and knocked on the door. "Come in," said a pleasant voice.

Sofia opened the door. In the middle of the room sat a beautiful woman. She was surrounded by plants, books, pictures, food, and old furniture, all in a wonderful mess. "Are you the Heartmender?" Sofia asked.

"I am your Heartmender," the woman answered. "Come and eat with me." Sofia hadn't noticed how hungry she was. She sat down in a big stuffed chair near the table. She ate a cheese sandwich and drank some hot cider.

"My name is Terra," the woman said. Her dark eyes shimmered.

Sofia reached into her bag, took out the halves of her heart, and gave them to Terra. Carefully, Terra cradled the pieces in her hands. She held them next to her own heart. "Come outside," she told Sofia. "Tonight is Crescent Moon. Your heart will be mended by moonlight."

Terra led Sofia down a narrow path through the trees. Sofia felt the soft earth under her feet and a gentle breeze on her face. The air smelled sweet. She could hear the wind speaking in the trees.

They stopped in front of a lake. In the moonlight, the lake was a silvery mirror. The dog was waiting for them.

Terra handed Sofia half of her heart. The dog turned his face towards the moon. Terra and Sofia fitted the heart halves together and lifted them up to the sky. A shimmering fine light traveled across the sky and touched Sofia's heart.

The wind whispered in her ears, the earth touched her feet, the lake mirrored the night sky. Sofia knew that all of these things were part of her, and she was part of them. She walked to the edge of the water and saw her own reflection. Her heart was whole again.

"Thank you, Heartmender," Sofia said.

erra was wearing a black clay necklace. She took it off and gave it to Sofia. "In this necklace, there is a bead for every star, the sun, and the moon," Terra explained. "There is a bead for every tree, flower, rock, and animal, and beads for all the different people that live on the earth. Wear it and you will never feel alone."

Terra smiled. "And if you ever get scared of the dark again, all you have to do is close your eyes. You will see your heart shine like the moon."

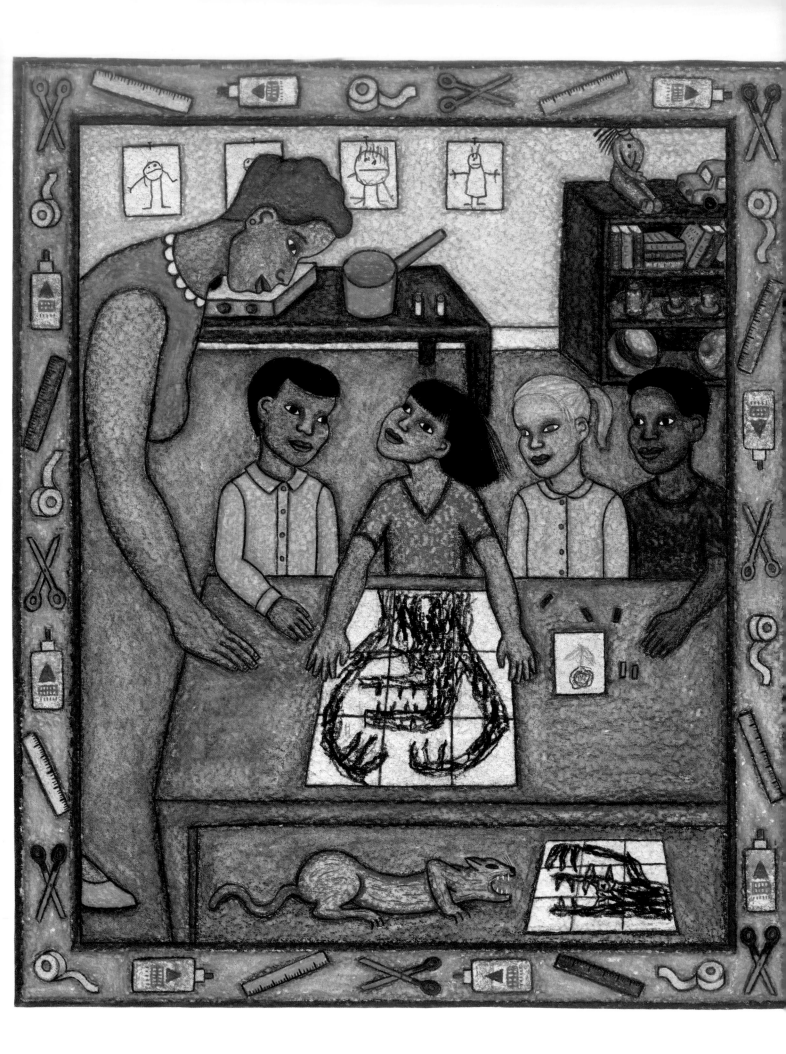

"Sofia, there you are! Come back inside and pick up your drawings!" Her teacher was calling her through the classroom window. Sofia looked down at the rock she was sitting on. Beside it, on the ground, was her school bag. She picked up her bag and walked back to the school.

Inside, Sofia gathered her drawings. Then she laid them out on the table. Side by side, like the pieces of a puzzle, they made one big shadow-monster. "I like my drawing," Sofia said proudly. "It's a shadow-monster."

The teacher and all the students were amazed that Sofia's drawings made one big picture. They admired her shadow-monster. Then they spent the rest of the day putting all of their drawings together into one big meadow full of spring flowers.

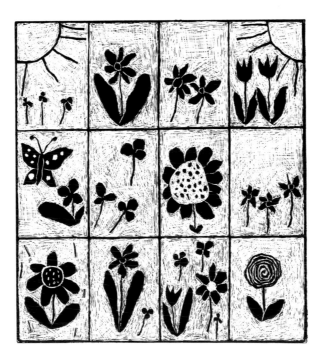

After school, Sofia brought home her shadow-monster picture and taped it to the refrigerator. Later, when her mother and father saw it, she told them, "This is a shadow-monster. It has been scaring me in my room at night. That's why I wanted my light on. I felt sad and alone when you didn't believe me."

Sofia's mother and father looked at the shadow-monster. They looked at Sofia. They looked at each other. "From now on, you can have your light on whenever you want," they said.

That night, when Sofia was getting ready for bed, she opened her school bag. Inside was the black clay necklace. She put it on and felt it grow warm against her skin. Then she looked out her window at the horizon.

"When the edge turns pink, the moon comes," she said to her cat. "We'd better turn the lamp off so we can see her shine."

Sofia and her cat climbed into their beds. Their room was bathed in moonlight all night long.

There is a light that shines beyond
all things on earth beyond us all
beyond the heavens
the very highest heavens
This is the light that shines in our Heart.

Chandogya Upanishad 3.13.7